32 Days

A Story of Faith and Courage

Written by Ellen Lucey Prozeller

Pauline
BOOKS & MEDIA
Boston

Library of Congress Cataloging-in-Publication Data

Names: Prozeller, Ellen Lucey.

Title: 32 days : a story of faith and courage / written by Ellen Lucey Prozeller.

Other titles: Thirty-two days

Description: Boston : Pauline Books & Media, 2016. | Summary: Archbishop Fulton J. Sheen relates the story of young Pei, whose devotion to the Blessed Sacrament in 1948 China, at the risk of her life, inspired him to spend more time with Jesus. Includes historical information, discussion questions, and glossary.

Identifiers: LCCN 2016012138| ISBN 9780819806574 (pbk.) | ISBN 0819806579 (pbk.)

Subjects: | CYAC: Christian life--Fiction. | Lord's Supper--Fiction. | Communism--Fiction. | Family life--China--Fiction. | Catholics--Fiction. | China--History--1949---Fiction. | Sheen, Fulton J. (Fulton John), 1895-1979--Fiction.

Classification: LCC PZ7.1.P785 Aah 2016 | DDC [Fic]--dc23

LC record available at https://lccn.loc.gov/2016012138

Design by Sr. Mary Joseph Peterson, FSP

Cover art by Carlotta Tormey

This is a fictionalized account based on the true story of an eleven-year-old Chinese girl who risked her life to visit Jesus in the Blessed Sacrament. The story also includes Archbishop Fulton J. Sheen. While Archbishop Sheen and the Chinese girl, whose name has been lost to history, are real historical figures, elements of this story are fictional products of the author's imagination.

"P" and PAULINE are registered trademarks of the Daughters of St. Paul.

Published by Pauline Books & Media, 50 Saint Pauls Avenue, Boston, MA 02130–3491

Printed in the U.S.A.

32D VSAUSAPEOILL2-110107 0657-9

www.pauline.org

Pauline Books & Media is the publishing house of the Daughters of St. Paul, an international congregation of women religious serving the Church with the communications media.

2 3 4 5 6 7 8 9   22 21 20 19 18

32 Days

This book is dedicated to

Ignatius Cardinal Kung Pin-Mei,

Venerable Archbishop Fulton J. Sheen,

and Our Lady of Sheshan

Contents

Introduction

Near the end of his life, Archbishop Fulton Sheen shared with a television journalist an event in a young Chinese girl's life that deeply inspired his prayer life. We know very little else about this young girl. Even her name is lost to history. But her courage and faith have not been forgotten. This book is a fictionalized account of Archbishop Sheen's interview and the shocking events in this young girl's life, which have inspired many people.

32 Days is not a history book, but it is a book about faith and courage. However, to understand the events that take place in this book, it is important to know a little about the history of China and the time in which this story occurs.

Christianity was first introduced to China in the seventh century by an Assyrian monk named Alopen. By 1700 there were about 200,000 Catholics in China. Unfortunately, the emperor at the time was angered that the Church did not allow certain native ceremonies, so he ordered all the missionaries to leave at once.

Then, in the 1800s things began to change. There was more Western influence in China, and Christianity had more freedom to spread. Many missionaries went to China to evangelize the people and establish churches and schools. During this period many people converted to the Catholic faith.

In the 1920s China was divided between two opposing political forces: the Nationalist Party and the Chinese Communist Party. On one side, the Nationalist leader, Chiang Kai-shek (Chee-ahng Kye-shek), with support from the United States, wanted the rich to maintain control, and he also wanted to modernize China. On the other side, the Communists, led by Mao Zedong (Maow Zuh-dohng) and supported by Russia, wanted a society without a ruling class and without religion.

Because they were promised a better life, many peasants supported the Communists. The Communists were able to take control—first of the countryside and then of the major cities —without much resistance. In 1949, Mao Zedong declared the beginning of the People's Republic of China.

The new Communist government forbade the practice of religion. Foreign-born priests and religious brothers and sisters were expelled from China. Those priests, brothers, and sisters who were born in China were imprisoned in harsh labor camps or sentenced to death if they continued to cling to their ministry and religious vocation.

The story of the girl who inspired Archbishop Sheen takes place in 1948 in a little village near Shanghai, China, just before the Communists took over the government.

Prologue

A white-haired bishop sat in an easy chair across from his interviewer in a small TV studio. This wasn't the first time he had been in front of the cameras. No. He had plenty of experience on his own television show, *Life Is Worth Living*. Known for his warmth and humor, Archbishop Fulton J. Sheen had been a very popular and influential TV personality in the 1950s and 1960s. His weekly show had been watched by millions of people, Catholic and non-Catholic alike. Archbishop Sheen had become famous for his ability to explain deep ideas in a simple way, often while writing on an ever-present blackboard. With a big smile on his face, he enjoyed bringing the Gospel to anyone willing to watch.

It was now 1979, and Archbishop Sheen felt just as at home on this production set as he had on his old one. With a sign from the director, the show began and so did the interview.

"It's an honor to welcome Archbishop Fulton Sheen to our show. Is this pretty much like the set you had on *Life Is Worth Living?*" asked the interviewer.

"Almost . . ." the archbishop responded with a chuckle. "But you're missing a very important part—the blackboard!"

"I'm afraid I don't have a blackboard, Archbishop Sheen. But as you can see and feel, we have plenty of studio lights."

"Yes," the archbishop agreed, wiping his brow. "They're certainly hot!"

"I remember your show, Archbishop Sheen. I bet we all do," said the interviewer while gesturing toward the studio audience. "In fact, I'd go so far as to say that you are perhaps the greatest and most beloved preacher of the twentieth century."

Archbishop Sheen smiled. "Don't stuff my head with such praise; it's big enough already! But seriously, I hope that people grew closer to God with the help of my show and that they never forget that the love of God—especially Jesus in the Holy Eucharist—is by far the most important thing to remember."

"Archbishop Sheen, you've met popes, bishops, priests, world leaders, and various holy men and women. Of all of them, who has inspired you the most?"

The archbishop did not think long before responding. With a twinkle in his eyes, he said, "You're right. I've been blessed to meet all kinds of famous and important people—but none of them inspired me more than a little Chinese girl. I never met her, but ever since I heard about her, she has inspired me to impress upon my listeners the importance of spending time with Jesus in the Blessed Sacrament and not taking him for granted."

"Really?" the interviewer asked, intrigued. "A little Chinese girl?"

"She was eleven years old," Archbishop Sheen began, "and in many ways she was just an ordinary girl. Yet her courage and love for Jesus in the Most Blessed Sacrament made her quite extraordinary. Would you like to hear her story?"

Chapter 1

Facing the Beast

The sun was bright, but Pei (Pay) was inside helping MaMa clean their small home in the countryside outside of Shanghai, China.

Pei looked out the window wistfully. *When will my chores be done so I can go play?* she wondered.

Because of the war, life was becoming more difficult for Pei's family. It seemed as though every day brought less time to play and more time for chores so her parents could provide food for their small family. Suddenly, Pei was startled out of her daydreaming.

"Take me out—now!" demanded Pei's little sister, Ling, with a stomp of her foot. "I want to go outside! Pleeeease?"

Pei shook her head. She had so much to do to help MaMa.

"Look," four-year-old Ling continued while pointing to her head. "I'm already wearing my warm hat."

"But I have chores to do," Pei explained, as she adjusted Ling's hat. "It *would* be nice to get some fresh air, though. I suppose we *could go* if we didn't stay too long. All right, let's ask MaMa!"

Ling clapped her chubby hands as Pei grabbed her hat. Holding hands, the two sisters left their small house with their mother's permission. The girls smiled as they breathed in the fresh, clean air.

"Aah," said Ling as she sniffed the air with her nose. "It smells nice out here. Not like our house!"

"Yes, it's lovely. And look over there, Ling! Let's get some stones. Do you want me to show you how to make them skip when we get to the pond?"

"Yeah!" said Ling, as she ran on short legs to the pile of stones nearby.

"Look for big, flat ones; they work best," added Pei. Once their pockets were filled, the two strolled on past the edge of the village and toward the pond.

"See the yellow and white flowers?" asked Pei, as she drew Ling's attention to a fragrant bush. "It's wintersweet, and it's MaMa's favorite. She likes it because it smells so good. I'm going to break some stems off for her."

While Pei was gathering the wintersweet branches, Ling ran ahead.

Hearing her sister's laugh, Pei looked up and called out, "Don't get so far ahead of me, Ling! You could get hurt or—"

Suddenly, the earth shook and the sound of thundering hooves drowned out Pei's voice.

"Ling!" shouted Pei, as a big, wild boar bared its tusks and raced toward her little sister.

The younger girl was filled with terror while Pei, heart pounding, sprinted to try and protect her. Although Pei hadn't heard of any recent wild boar attacks, her parents had always warned her to flee from the dangerous animals. Pei scooped up Ling and froze. The huge animal was nearly upon them!

"Leave us alone!" Pei yelled as she held a trembling Ling tight.

Ling hid her tear-soaked face in her sister's neck. Pei could smell the beast's stench. Its fierce eyes flashed and its sharp tusks dripped with thick, white drool. Pei's mind was racing. *O God, what do I do? Help us!* Quickly, hardly thinking, Pei reached down, grasped a handful of dirt, and threw it at the charging boar.

The cloud of dirt covered the boar's face, startling but not stopping him. Angrier than ever, the boar backed up, lowered his head, and charged the sisters. Convinced that they had only moments to live, Pei grabbed the first stone she found in her pocket and hurled it at the animal. Then Pei scrunched her eyes shut and turned her back to the beast, hoping to protect her sister. *"Jesus, save us!"* she prayed.

The boar's low growl suddenly changed to a high pitched squeal. Pei had hit her target! Opening her eyes and turning, Pei saw the beast run back into the woods. She sighed in relief, and dropped to the ground with Ling still in her arms.

"Thank you, Jesus," Pei whispered. "Thank you."

Chapter 2

The Communists Are Near

Breathless, with cheeks red from running in the chilly air, the girls burst through the door to their home.

"Oh, MaMa!" Pei cried, throwing her arms around MaMa's neck. "I've never been so happy to be home! We barely escaped! God protected us!"

"What?!" asked MaMa, who quickly put down her embroidery work to look at her daughters.

"MaMa, a big, stinky, ugly animal wanted to eat us!" said Ling.

"Good heavens, girls, what happened?" cried MaMa.

"We were going to skip some stones by the pond when suddenly—" began Pei.

"A big, ugly, stinky thing came running at us. He would have eaten us, too, if Pei hadn't saved us," Ling added, with a huge smile on her face.

"Well, thank God he didn't! I can't even imagine losing you girls." MaMa hugged them, and said with tears in her eyes, "I am just so happy and grateful to God for keeping you safe. Tonight we will pray in thanksgiving as a family."

After Pei and Ling's older brother, Min, and BaBa, their father, came home, Ling retold the whole story. This time she pounded her feet on the floor to make the thundering sound and put her hands near her mouth to look like long tusks.

"And he was so ugly!" she said. "I was brave, though. Pei said so."

"I'm sure you were," said Min, "but it was Pei who saved the day."

"No," Pei put in quietly. "Jesus saved us both."

"You're right, of course," BaBa said, "but your quick thinking helped. You're a very brave girl, Pei," he said, patting the top of her head. "But we have more dangerous things to discuss."

"*More* danger?" asked MaMa, her face lined with worry.

"I'm afraid so. A couple arrived from Shanghai today and told some of us about the ongoing civil war between the Nationalist Party and the Communist Party."

"What did they say?" asked MaMa.

"They said the Communists are winning the battle for control of the country."

"I'm glad we don't live closer to Shanghai!" Min exclaimed.

"The fighting doesn't just involve those who live in Shanghai, son. We're all affected by it, or will be," explained BaBa.

"Everyone at church is so frightened about what might happen," MaMa added. "Some of the women said the Communist army even evacuated a few villages near the Basilica of Our Lady of Sheshan (Sheh-shahn). They think they can stop people from going there to pray."

Pei remembered her parents telling her how the Chinese people in the area of Shanghai gave the Virgin Mary the title of Our Lady of Sheshan because the basilica built in her honor was near Mount Sheshan. As Pei listened to her mother, she felt sadness wash over her. She knew that the basilica was special to the people; they trusted in Mary to pray for them.

"The Communists don't believe in God, and they don't want anyone else to believe either. A lot of people will probably stop visiting the basilica. They may be so afraid that they'll even stop going to church altogether," BaBa said, somberly.

"BaBa," began Pei, "do you really think things are going to change that much?"

"Yes, Pei, I do. People are desperate for a better life," BaBa answered. "Just look at our little village. No one has money to buy clothes or fix their houses. We certainly don't have much, but there are many families with even less."

"The Communists have promised food and work and other good things. Many people believe them," said MaMa, wringing her hands. "But people don't realize what the Communists will take. There may be no place for freedom or faith in China anymore."

"I hope they forget about our little village," said Min.

Shrugging her shoulders, Ling reasoned, "Maybe we're so small they won't find us."

Smiling at the youngest child in the family, BaBa said, "I don't think the size of our village will matter much to them. Mr. Liang has a sister who lives in Shanghai with her family. She told him that the Communists are mistreating Christians, and they're closing churches because they reject the existence of God."

"How can they not believe in God?" asked Pei. "Don't they know that God loves them?"

BaBa looked at her and nodded, "That's just it, Pei. They don't believe in God."

"That's so sad, BaBa. I'm afraid of what will happen if they come here," added Pei.

"Children, we trust God. We can ask him to help us and all our neighbors. We can also ask God to show the Communists his truth," BaBa said, confidently.

"Let's ask Our Lady of Sheshan to pray with us and for us," MaMa suggested.

Ling went to sit on MaMa's lap, and together the family prayed the Rosary. They prayed in thanksgiving for Pei and Ling having survived the boar attack. They also prayed for their fellow villagers and that the Communists would stop hurting Christians.

After praying, Pei and Ling went to sleep on the bed they shared. The thin mattress, on top of a wooden plank and low to the ground, was covered with warm blankets. Ling fell asleep right away, but Pei's mind would not rest.

What will the Communists do to us if they come here? Pei wondered. *Will they take our food? Will they close our church?*

Chapter 3

NaiNai and YeYe

"Look, it's YeYe (Yeh-yeh) and NaiNai! (Nye-nye)" cried Ling, her pigtails flying behind her. Ling and Pei had been waiting by the side of the road for their grandparents.

Pei remembered the long two-hour walk to her grandparents' small home in the hilly countryside. She had spent part of the previous summer with them helping to work the fields. Plowing, planting, hoeing, and watering in the hot sun was backbreaking work. When she remembered it, Pei could still taste the dust in her mouth and feel the sun burn her skin. Still, the meager crops of cabbage, carrot, sweet potato, and green onion were needed.

"Do you think they brought us something yummy to eat?" Ling wondered aloud, interrupting Pei's thoughts.

"I hope so, but don't you dare ask them about food, Ling! No one has enough," warned Pei. "I'm just happy that they traveled so far to spend Christmas with us." Then with a smile she added, "Now come on, let's go say hello to them!"

As the girls ran happily down the dusty road toward their grandmother, Ling called out to her, "NaiNai!"

From where she sat on the cart NaiNai waved at her granddaughters. Pei could see lots of cabbages surrounding the smiling woman. There was even enough to share with some of the neighbors!

Once they got home, MaMa helped NaiNai climb down from the cart while the girls helped YeYe unload the cabbages. Soon BaBa and Min joined the happy reunion.

"Oh, it's so good to see you!" said NaiNai, looking at MaMa. "The children have grown since I last saw them!"

"Look at Min. He's almost a man!" said YeYe. Then turning to his grandson he added, "Only another year or two at school, then you'll be a worker, like your father and me!"

Min gasped while the girls giggled. *It's hard to imagine my brother as a man,* thought Pei.

"Come, let's go inside," MaMa said, interrupting Pei's thoughts. "NaiNai and YeYe should rest after such a long trip."

NaiNai and YeYe slowly walked into the house. Finding a chair at the table, NaiNai took a seat and sighed. "Ah, that's better. The trip seems longer the older I get." A big smile graced her slender face.

"Here," MaMa said, "have some fresh tea." With that Pei quietly filled the beautifully decorated teapot with steaming water and fragrant tea leaves and placed it next to MaMa.

"I should not complain though; I got to sit in the cart while your YeYe pushed it almost the entire way!" said NaiNai, as she watched MaMa pour the tea through a small handheld strainer into a delicate cup. "It's YeYe who bore the heavy burden."

"Oh, you're never a burden, little wife," said YeYe, smiling at her. "As long as God gives me the strength I need, I won't complain. After all, I'm not yet sixty years of age, and you are younger still!"

After the family enjoyed their tea, YeYe, BaBa, and Min spoke in one corner of the room about the harvest while Pei helped MaMa and NaiNai wash the dishes.

"Did you run into any trouble on the way here?" said MaMa in a low voice.

"No, thank God. But we did see some refugees fleeing from areas where there is heavy fighting," NaiNai said. "The Communists seem to be winning many of the battles. May God have mercy!"

Overhearing the conversation, YeYe joined the two women. "The Communists will make peasants of everyone!" he said.

"Enough talk of politics!" MaMa said, standing up. "We'll end up with upset stomachs and we won't enjoy the fresh cabbage you've brought. Pei, can you and Ling please start to prepare a head of cabbage for tonight's supper?"

"Of course, MaMa," responded Pei, with a small bow. Tugging her sister along, Pei went just outside the house to where two buckets sat filled with well water. Pei filled a large bowl with the cool water from one of the buckets and set it on a rough wooden table outside the back door.

"The cabbages NaiNai and YeYe brought look so yummy!" exclaimed Ling as she watched her sister wash and then begin to cut one into strips.

"It's so nice to have fresh food! I can hardly wait for dinner so we can eat!" added Pei with a small smile.

"We were happy to bring the vegetables to you," said NaiNai, as she and MaMa joined the girls outside.

"One thing I miss is having rice every day," Pei sighed.

MaMa's face grew wistful. "Yes, prices for food have been so high. Many things have changed. Remember when beautiful garments hung here, all about the workroom? How colorful they were!"

Turning to Pei, MaMa said, "BaBa used to be so busy making clothing—capes, jackets, and even fine tunics—for the wealthy landowners of the district."

"Oh yes," replied NaiNai. "I remember the great fuss when the rich people came to order their jackets and tunics and beautiful *qipaos* (chee-pows). The glorious colors of those long, fitted dresses were dazzling. You brewed tea for them and used your best cups, too. Oh, those were happy days!"

Pei remembered wandering around the workshop when she was little, admiring the brightly colored silks, linens, and satins. She loved to run her small hands over the fine fabrics and trace the embroidered designs with her fingers. Nowadays there was almost no work for BaBa. People made do with what they had, stitching patches on worn elbows and knees.

"Did you do a lot of embroidery then, MaMa? On the rich people's clothes?" asked Pei, as she put the chopped cabbage back in the bowl.

"Your mother's skill with a needle was unmatched," said NaiNai. "No one could make dragons and butterflies as well as she did. They almost looked like they were alive."

"How I loved to decorate clothing like that!" MaMa said with a smile.

"Well, those days are in the past. Now we must plant and harvest our meager crops if we hope to eat," NaiNai said, somberly. There was worry in NaiNai and MaMa's eyes and a grim silence hung in the air.

Chapter 4

An Unexpected Gift

"Just cut it!" Pei urged her friend, Jiang-Mei (Jee-yang May). The two girls had been friends since they were little. The woods nearby were a favorite place for both of them. "How can you be afraid of a plant? It's only holly!"

"I'm not afraid of it, but it hurts!" Jiang-Mei said. "If you think it's so easy, why don't *you* cut it? You're the one who wants it to decorate your house for Christmas!"

"Fine," Pei replied as she reached over to carefully cut several branches with a small knife. Then Pei got up, dropped the knife, and chased Jiang-Mei with the branches. "But now . . . you're not safe from *me*!" she shouted.

The two girls chased each other all over the woods, laughing and jumping out from behind trees, and running in different directions. When they stopped to catch their breath, Jiang-Mei asked, "Pei, is your family going to use all the holly you've cut?"

"Why?" responded Pei. "Do you need some?"

"No, I just came to keep you company; my brother already gathered some for us. But the Lam family is Catholic; they would be happy if you gave some to them," Jiang-Mei told her.

With that Pei cut some extra branches.

When Pei returned home she had a surprise. "Look, everyone, come see what I got!" She held out some eggs and a small bag of rice.

"That's wonderful," NaiNai said. "Where did these treasures come from?"

"From our neighbors!" Pei responded happily. "Jiang-Mei told me that the Lam family needed some holly. When I went to give them a couple of branches, Mrs. Lam gave me an egg to thank us."

"Well, that explains one egg. What about the rest?" asked MaMa. "You didn't beg for food, did you, Pei?"

"No, MaMa, I didn't ask anyone for food," Pei said. "I cut enough holly to share with the Lams and our neighbors. They gave me the food as a thank-you," she explained.

"This will certainly help feed us all for the week. Thank God for his providence and care," replied MaMa as she made the Sign of the Cross.

Everyone bowed their head. *Thank you, God, for all you have given us,* Pei prayed quietly.

After the family had eaten their dinner that night, NaiNai told everyone with a big smile, "I have a surprise. Close your eyes now and I'll show you . . ."

Pei could hear NaiNai's shuffling feet as she left the room and returned.

"All right, open your eyes!" There, sitting on a stool in the middle of the family, was NaiNai with bundles of something wrapped in packing paper.

"What are they?" asked Min.

NaiNai carefully unwrapped each treasure and revealed the loveliest Christmas figurines. Pei watched as small statues of Mary, Joseph, the baby Jesus, angels, shepherds, sheep, and a cow emerged.

Ling clapped her hands. "They're so beautiful, NaiNai. Where did you get them?"

"They're very old. My father brought them back from Shanghai when I was about Pei's age. He said they came by ship all the way from Europe."

"Oh," continued Ling, "Mary is so pretty!"

"Baby Jesus is beautiful, too," said Pei in awe. "I wish I could hold him forever!"

"Do you really?"

"Oh, yes! But my arms would get tired."

"Pei, we can hold Jesus in our hearts instead of our hands. And there's a very special way to do that," responded NaiNai, as she patted Pei's hand. "I'll show you tomorrow."

"Children, it's time for bed," MaMa announced.

After the children were in bed, BaBa took MaMa aside and said, "I am glad the Lams gave us food. But I am worried we will not continue to have enough, especially now that YeYe and NaiNai are staying here. It isn't going to be easy to feed all of us."

MaMa looked tenderly at her husband. He had circles under his concerned eyes. She knew that BaBa slept poorly each night, worrying about whether there would be enough food for the family.

"The two of us will just keep doing what we've been doing," said MaMa. "We'll eat a little less. And God will provide. Look what he brought us today."

Then BaBa took MaMa's hands and prayed quietly, "Lord God, please help us to provide for our family. Help all the families who are struggling like we are. We trust you, Heavenly Father, but we are not sure if we have enough strength to get through this. Give us the faith we need to know that you are with us—even if things get worse. Amen."

Chapter 5

Pei Visits Jesus

The next day, with a cane in one hand and the other on Pei's shoulder, NaiNai and Pei walked slowly on the unpaved road. At the end of the road, near the entrance to the village, stood a small wooden church.

"Is that where we're going, NaiNai?" Pei asked, as she pointed to the village's church.

NaiNai nodded quietly as they continued to approach the building.

"Why are we going to the church?"

"I want to teach you how to pray," said NaiNai.

"But I already know how to pray. I've memorized all the prayers in my prayer book, and I can pray the Rosary too," declared Pei. "I pray a lot already, NaiNai," she continued. "Can I go play with Jiang-Mei instead?"

"Pei, you can go play if you would like, but don't you want to know what we are going to do?" asked NaiNai patiently.

Pei thought a moment. She was not sure she wanted to learn more about prayer, but she *did* want to spend more time with her grandmother.

"Yes, NaiNai, I want to learn," said Pei.

"Remember how you thought the little Baby Jesus I brought looked so beautiful?" NaiNai asked.

"Yes, NaiNai," Pei answered, not sure where the conversation was going.

"The Baby Jesus is lovely, but it's only a statue. The real Jesus is even more beautiful. We're going to visit him."

"What do you mean? My religion teacher, Sister Elizabeth, said that Jesus ascended into heaven after he rose from the dead. We can't go there," Pei said.

"Yes, we can, Pei. Sometimes, I spend an hour with Jesus in the tabernacle. It's called adoration," NaiNai replied.

"So you sit in church for a whole hour?" Pei wondered aloud.

"It's more than just sitting there," NaiNai assured her. "Jesus is always present in the tabernacle. He waits there for me, for you, for anyone who comes. I talk to him about anything and everything."

They continued to walk toward the church in silence.

"What do you mean, 'talk to him'?" Pei blurted out.

"Well, you talk to me, don't you? And you talk to your family and your friends at school, right?" her grandmother asked.

"Yes, of course, NaiNai. But talking to Jesus is different," Pei said, thoughtfully. "Jesus is God. I can't talk to him like he is just anyone. I can't tell him about my problems. I can't joke with him. I can't be angry at him."

"Oh Pei, that's where you're wrong," NaiNai said, shaking her head. "The good Lord already knows every thought, plan, dream, fear, and problem you've ever had. There's nothing you can't tell him. He *wants* you to talk to him because *you're* important to him."

"But I would have to be very serious if I was talking to God," continued Pei. "And I would have to use big, fancy words. I wouldn't know what to say or do."

"Jesus wants to be your friend, Pei. Just sit with him and tell him you love him. You can tell him about things that worry you and ask him what you should do. You can also thank him," her grandmother said, as she reached for the door. "There's so much to be grateful for. For example, today you could thank him for saving you and Ling from the boar. Talk to Jesus like you talk to your friends. The things you talk to Jiang-Mei about you can also share with him."

"Well, I guess I could try," Pei said, as they entered the church and blessed themselves with holy water.

NaiNai kissed the top of Pei's head. "Jesus will show you how to pray a holy hour, Pei. Just open your heart to him and let him fill it for you." With that NaiNai led her to a pew in the front. Pei quickly genuflected and stepped in. "You pray here, near the font where you were baptized. That was such a happy day! The priest gave you the Christian name 'Lucy,' to honor a very brave saint. She is a special friend in heaven for you, Pei. You can always ask her to pray for you."

"I can?" Pei asked quietly.

"Of course. That is how the saints help us," NaiNai answered, smiling as she moved a few pews away. "I will pray here. I want to have my own conversation with my best friend. Tell Jesus everything that is on your mind, and I will too. Talk to him about the people you love, the things you're sorry for, and how much you love and adore him. Then listen. You won't hear him with your ears. But he will speak to you in your heart and in your mind."

As NaiNai made her way to another pew, Pei folded her hands and looked at the tabernacle. The red candle near it was glowing brightly. She knew that Jesus was there, just as NaiNai had said, waiting for her to visit him. Then Pei closed her eyes and prayed:

Hi, Jesus. I hope I'm doing this right. NaiNai said I should just talk to you about everything, so I'm trying. Yesterday I said I wished I could hold you forever. And I do, because I love you a lot. But I also want you to hold me. Sometimes I'm frightened—like when the boar charged us. Sometimes I feel sad because MaMa and BaBa worry about not having enough money or food. I worry about NaiNai and YeYe. And I'm worried about what will happen if the Communists come.

Then Pei sat and listened. . . .

ॐ

"Come, Pei. It's time to go home now," NaiNai whispered.

"But I thought you said we were staying here for an hour," replied Pei.

"It's been more than an hour, child," NaiNai said. "Your mother will be waiting for us."

As they left the church Pei smiled and said, "I feel better now, NaiNai. More peaceful."

"Yes, that is what happens when we bring our problems to Jesus," NaiNai said.

Chapter 6

Christmas Day

It was morning before school started and the Catholic children in the village had gathered for their religion classes before regular class with their teacher, *Sifu* (See-foo) Yang began.

"Children, since tomorrow is Christmas, I've asked Father Anthony to tell you a little about how he celebrated Christmas when he was growing up in New Jersey in the United States of America," said Sister Elizabeth, a young sister originally from Shanghai.

"Good morning, children," began Father Anthony. "As many of you know, I grew up in the United States, but I have lived here in China for many years."

Father Anthony, usually smiling and happy, had seemed troubled lately. He looked like he had not slept well for a long time.

"In many places all over the world, the churches have choirs and bells and a Christmas Mass at midnight. Christmas is celebrated by almost everyone. Stores and schools are closed; people stay home from work; and all the city streets are decorated."

"I wish that's how it was here in China," said one of the boys.

"Perhaps someday it will be," Sister Elizabeth interjected. "But in the meantime, our Christmas is special, too. Our Mass will be early enough for all of your families to attend. And we'll have *dim sum*, dumplings, and rice cakes together."

"Yum," the children all said in unison.

Sister Elizabeth continued, "Now let's cut out our paper lanterns for tomorrow's Christmas Mass."

{∞}

Pei's whole family gathered toward the front of the small, brown, wooden church. Pei sat between her brother and sister, beaming with joy. Candles were glowing; holly sprays dressed the altar. Although no one had been able to buy or make anything new in quite a while, everyone in the small church wore their best clothing. The parish Christmas nativity set had been placed on a table beside the altar. It was a lovely set made of bamboo with bits of colored glass. BaBa had donated some pretty silver cloth to adorn it. The whole parish had been waiting for days for the statue of Baby Jesus to take its place. The Lord had come into the world!

Father Anthony entered in white vestments representing purity and holiness, and then everyone sang, *O Come, All Ye Faithful*. The Mass of Christmas morning began.

After Mass, everyone gathered together to celebrate. All the families of the parish had brought whatever food they could to make it special. MaMa and NaiNai were in charge of the tea, so Pei and Min had woken early to carry the water. *Sifu* Yang, the village's only schoolteacher, had made delicious rice cakes. All of the parishioners gathered around chairs and tables with their tea and food. Pei sat next to Father Anthony and said, "Tell us more about Christmas when you were little, Father."

Father smiled, remembering. "It was wonderful! We all went to Midnight Mass, even the children, and then we'd walk home through the cold, snowy streets to a big delicious dinner. Our family was all together, and then we'd exchange presents. Finally, we'd fall into bed and the next morning there would be toys under the Christmas tree. We had such fun!"

"You must miss your family and all the good things you had in America," MaMa said.

"Yes, but all of you here are my family too. This is where God has called me to serve him as a priest, and I wouldn't change it for the world."

After they had eaten, Sister Elizabeth passed out red paper and string to all the children. Ling and Min made dragon kites, which they flew in the open field. Even though it was chilly, soon many other children joined them.

"Let's see how high we can go, Ling," Min said. The kites were like great flying dragons soaring in the bright blue sky. Pei thought she had never seen anything lovelier. The chirping of birds, the sound of the nearby trickling brook, and the children's laughter were the only sounds. Everything in the village was calm. Suddenly, from a distance, loud noises could be heard.

"What is that noise?" MaMa asked Father Anthony.

"I'm not sure," he responded.

"Could it be an airplane?" YeYe asked.

"Perhaps people celebrating from other villages?" suggested NaiNai.

At first, no one knew what the noise was, but soon enough it became clear. Trucks. Many trucks rolled into the village square.

"Remain calm, comrades," a loud voice said, coming over the crackling speakers mounted on one of the military vehicles. "We were ordered here by General Mao Zedong. He will restore China to its greatness!"

Sister Elizabeth quickly gathered the children and brought them back to their families. Pei ran to her mother's side. The joyful smile that had been there was gone; worry had replaced it. Pei began to feel anxious as she looked around; no one was smiling.

"Go to your jobs and classrooms at once and resume your day," the voice over the loudspeakers commanded. "You and your children will remember this as a great day for the people. Long live the revolution! Long live China!"

The Communists had arrived.

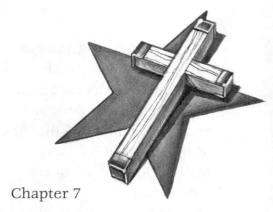

Chapter 7

Captain Chen's Brutality

The next morning seemed like any other day. The birds sang. The sun shone. The air was cool and crisp. No one would have guessed that six trucks had entered the village the day before, grinding their wheels into the rutted, dusty road.

But soon it became clear that everything was changing. Soldiers with angry faces flooded the village streets, marched around, and made a show of "inspecting" deserted tea shops and stores. Just to show their power, they lopped off low-hanging tree branches with their knives and kicked tame ducks that wandered where people usually gathered or walked. Those who could, stayed home, but most adults had work that needed to be done and the children had to go to school.

"Good morning, children," Sister Elizabeth greeted the class with a smile. "We had a lovely Christmas Mass yesterday, and it was nice having fun and eating afterward as well."

"I ate two rice cakes after Mass, Sister," said Jiang-Mei. "Did you have any?"

Before Sister Elizabeth could respond, one of the boys at the back of the classroom interrupted. "Excuse me, Sister. The rice cakes are all gone, but the soldiers and trucks are still here."

"All right children . . . first, Jiang-Mei, we *did* have delicious rice cakes with our tea," replied Sister Elizabeth. "And, you're right," she added, turning her attention to the boy. "The Communist soldiers *are* still here. I know you must all have questions about what the soldiers are doing here and what is happening, but I don't have any answers for you." Sister Elizabeth looked at the anxious faces around her. A flicker of worry crossed her face, but then she smiled. Adjusting her grey habit and white veil, Sister continued, "But when we're afraid, worried, or feel like we're alone, we can pray and ask God for courage and strength. Now, who would like to lead us in the Our Father?"

After prayers, Sister Elizabeth began the lesson. "How many of you have heard about guardian angels?" Several hands went up. "Every person who believes has a guardian angel. Our angels guide us and stay with us our whole lives."

"If angels are guarding us, why do bad things still happen?" asked Pei.

"That's a good question. Let me see if I can explain," Sister Elizabeth answered. "God loves all people. But people have free will and can choose to do either good or bad things."

"Maybe God should kill all the bad people," added another boy.

"But God is love," Sister Elizabeth reminded her class. "Instead of killing people who choose to do evil, God never stops inviting them to listen to him and do good. This is how Jesus treated those he loved. What God wants most of all is for *everyone* to choose to freely love him and live with him in heaven."

SLAM!

The classroom door flew open and banged into the wall behind it. A Communist officer followed by six soldiers carrying guns stormed into the classroom. The officer looked at the children and then glared at Sister Elizabeth. He put his right hand on his hip, next to his holstered pistol.

"I am Captain Chen, an officer of the People's Liberation Army," he barked. "Stand when I enter a room!"

Pointing to Sister Elizabeth, the captain continued, "I caught you red-handed lying to these foolish children. Filling their minds with fairy tales and complete nonsense. . . . You are nothing but a traitor to China!"

Shocked, Sister Elizabeth replied quietly, "With respect, I am not a traitor, sir. I am an honorable Chinese woman." Pei noticed that Sister Elizabeth nervously touched the rosary beads at her waist.

The officer moved toward the young sister. Putting his face right in front of hers, he shouted, "Silence, traitor!" Spit flew from his mouth. He then reached over and yanked her rosary beads, causing them to scatter all over the wooden floor.

All the children's eyes grew wide with fear. Pei's mouth was dry and she realized she was shaking. She reached for Jiang-Mei's hand and found her best friend was shaking too. No one had ever acted that way toward a sister in their presence before.

Sister Elizabeth stood alone at the front of the classroom, but her face looked determined. *What will these men do to her?* Pei asked herself. *I've got to do something to help her.* In the next moment Pei broke free from Jiang-Mei and ran to Sister Elizabeth's side.

Pei looked up to catch Sister Elizabeth's eyes. Then pain jolted through her. The officer smacked the side of Pei's head so hard that she fell to the floor.

"You!" he shouted. "You are nothing but an ignorant dog. You have allowed yourself to be fooled by this deceiver. Led around like an animal on a leash."

Captain Chen turned his attention back to Sister Elizabeth. "You tell these children foolish tales about a god that doesn't exist!" he accused. "You must be very stupid yourself, if you believe your own lies. You will be sent where you can do no more harm, traitor."

Two soldiers grabbed Sister Elizabeth by the arms and forced her from the room. But as she was being taken away, she turned to her students and said loudly, "Have faith in Jesus, children!" Before she could say anything else the soldiers pushed her roughly through the classroom door.

The frightened children cried silently. Jiang-Mei went over to Pei and helped her up. "Those who allowed this traitor to teach lies will also be punished," said Captain Chen. "This is no longer Traitor Yang's classroom. Tomorrow you will have a *good* teacher, a *sifu* who is loyal to China, a patriot." Then he ordered the children outside.

Standing by the road the children saw soldiers with their guns aimed at Sister Elizabeth and *Sifu* Yang. One by one the women were roughly pushed into the back of a military truck. Two armed soldiers followed them, and the tailgate was slammed shut. A guard standing near the children said, "Let this be a lesson to you. Traitors with foreign ideas and customs have no place in China!"

Chapter 8

Comrade Zhao

Pei, her friends, and some of the people in the village who had heard the commotion watched as the truck sped away down the road. As Pei fought the tears that welled up in her eyes, she wondered what would happen to Sister Elizabeth and *Sifu* Yang. Then Pei remembered that Sister had just said that prayer is important when you are feeling upset. Pei began to pray.

Father in heaven, please help us. I am scared. Everyone is scared. Please give Sister Elizabeth, Sifu Yang, and all of us the courage and strength we need. Please help me, Jesus.

Pei's prayer was interrupted when Captain Chen shouted more orders. Immediately the Communist soldiers went back into the school and brought out the crucifix Sister Elizabeth had hung on the wall, along with some religious pictures and a small statue of Jesus. The soldiers threw the crucifix and statue to the ground. Then they ripped the holy pictures into several pieces and scattered them. Pei could feel her sore head throbbing. She thought of Sister Elizabeth's rosary beads on the floor, but was too frightened to retrieve them. Captain Chen told one of the soldiers to guard the school, and then he left with the rest of the soldiers.

"What do we do now?" Min whispered. No one answered. The children just stood, too shocked to move or make sense of what had happened.

The guard began to laugh. "What are you waiting for? You heard the captain. Your new *sifu* will be here tomorrow. Go home!"

⋙⋘

The next day, Pei prepared for school with a knot in her stomach.

"Just do what you are told, Pei, and try not to say too much. Jesus is with you, he will give you courage," assured MaMa.

Pei nodded silently. Her head still hurt and she missed Sister Elizabeth and *Sifu* Yang.

When Pei and the other children entered the one-room school house it was different. Red banners—for the People's Liberation Army and the Communist Party—had been hung around the room, as well as a picture of their leader, Mao Zedong. The portrait took the place of honor at the front of the classroom. The five-pointed red star, a symbol of Communism, decorated flags, the soldiers' uniforms, shops, and public spaces.

Somber-faced children waited for their new teacher to arrive. After what seemed like an eternity, a straight-backed woman entered the room. The children immediately stood up. Everything about their new teacher was sharp, from her bony shoulders and knees to the shape of her face. She was dressed in black with a giant red star pinned to her jacket. When she smiled, her dark, piercing eyes remained cold.

Pei looked over at her brother. Min stood straight, but by the way he gripped the chair in front of him, Pei knew that he was as nervous as she was. All the children waited quietly for the teacher to speak.

Clapping her hands, the new teacher drew the children's attention. As she stood in the center of the room she said, in a nasally voice, "I am Comrade Zhao (Jhaow). In my class, you will learn all about our illustrious country. We are strong and supreme in the world. One day we will show the whole world what China can do."

Comrade Zhao moved around the room with arms clasped behind her back. Once she reached the front of the room, she stood by the small wooden desk. On the desk were two wooden bowls. From the first bowl Comrade Zhao took red stars made out of fabric.

"You must always wear the red stars our country is giving you," she said, as she walked up and down the aisle passing out the little stars to each of the children. "They are a sign that you are loyal to China."

Using the straight pin that was attached to the star, Pei quietly fastened the star to her blouse. Once again standing by the desk, the teacher pointed to the other bowl. "You will receive these small bags of rice at the end of class today. You are to bring them to your families as proof of the goodness and generosity of our Great Leader Chairman Mao and the Communist Party."

Comrade Zhao led the children in their lessons in mathematics, writing, and reading as usual, but then she read from a new book. The new book talked about certain warlords, the Nationalists, foreigners, and other groups the Communists had defeated.

Just before the children were to eat their lunch, Comrade Zhao recited some of Mao Zedong's words. Then she said, "Some of you have been exposed to lies from foreigners. These lies are no longer tolerated in this classroom or anywhere in the new People's Republic of China. Instead, you will learn wisdom from our leader."

The children were then instructed to stand and face the picture of Mao Zedong. They listened to his words as Comrade Zhao spoke them. To Pei, they sounded like angry words.

"Our god is the Chinese people. Together we can clear away the mountains of oppression that weigh us down," she proclaimed in a loud voice.

"Now, you will repeat these words until you have memorized them," the new teacher instructed. The class recited the words until it was time to leave. "We will learn from our leader every day. This is being done in schools throughout our great nation," said Comrade Zhao, proudly.

At the end of the school day, Pei and Min ran home as quickly as they could. They were anxious to tell their parents about Comrade Zhao. When they took their shoes off at the door, Ling ran to greet them.

"Where are MaMa and BaBa?" Min asked, lifting his little sister up into the air.

"They aren't here. A man came this morning and told them they had to be pro . . . pro . . . protive."

"You mean, pro*duct*ive?" Min questioned.

"I don't remember," Ling said, shyly. "But NaiNai and YeYe are here."

"NaiNai!" Pei called out. Her grandmother came in from washing the vegetables.

"I'm here, Pei. There's no need to shout," NaiNai replied calmly.

"But where are MaMa and BaBa? What is going on? Everything is changing!" Pei exclaimed. YeYe looked up from the newspaper he had been reading.

"Hush, Pei!" YeYe warned. "MaMa and BaBa are okay. They will be back this evening. Things are changing everywhere. We have to be careful about what we say. The Communists might hear us."

"But we're home now," Pei said.

"I'm not sure that matters anymore," said NaiNai sadly.

Chapter 9

An Attack in Church

For the rest of the week, Pei and her class-mates struggled to settle into their new routine with Comrade Zhao. Just as their teacher had told them, the children recited Chairman Mao Zedong's sayings every day.

Another thing they were required to do was exercise. Under the watchful eye of their teacher, the students marched, carrying sticks over their shoulders as if they were rifles. As the students marched back and forth, Comrade Zhao would shout more of Chairman Mao's sayings. One of Comrade Zhao's favorites was: "Be brave. Do not fear sacrifice. We can overcome all difficulties."

One day blended into the next. Pei was grate-ful when Sunday came.

ා

Huan (Hwahn) pulled on the rope to ring the bell. As altar server, it was his job to remind villagers about Sunday Mass.

When Huan got to the bottom of the stairs, he noticed Father Anthony peeking through the sacristy door. "It looks like fewer people have come to Mass today," the priest said sadly.

"They're frightened, Father Anthony," replied Huan. "Even my family is scared to come. They saw what happened to Sister Elizabeth and *Sifu* Yang."

"I am offering this Mass for Sister Elizabeth and *Sifu* Yang. I know everyone is worried that the same thing will happen to them. I'm worried too. But all we can do is put our faith in our Divine Savior."

When the clock chimed the hour, Father Anthony and Huan stepped out of the sacristy to begin Mass. As Father Anthony bowed to kiss the altar, he heard commotion break out in the back of the church. When the priest turned around to see what was happening, he saw many soldiers. They were stampeding down the center aisle, drowning out the hymn. They were led by Captain Chen, the officer who had all the medals on his uniform. The soldiers had heavy sticks in their hands and most had guns in their holsters.

Father Anthony moved toward the soldiers. "What is going on here?" he demanded. "This is the house of God! Show some respect!"

"You know nothing about respect, priest," Captain Chen replied. "I'll give you a lesson in respect." Two of the soldiers stood in back at the doors. The rest moved forward and into the sanctuary.

The people in the pews were too stunned to move at first. When several tried to get out of their seats and approach the altar, the soldiers beat them back with clubs. In a few minutes, all was silent. Captain Chen breathed in deeply. Then he proceeded to speak.

"All of you people are fools!" he spat out. "Summoned by bells like mindless schoolchildren! And to what? Superstition and nonsense! You have been listening to these so-called wise priests and missionaries who want to fill your empty heads with foreign imperialism. Don't you understand? They want you to be their slaves. In the new China we will have no foreign masters!"

Captain Chen nodded to the men standing nearest to him. In a moment, Father Anthony's arms were pinned behind his back by two of the soldiers.

"Lord, have mercy! God, forgive them!" Father Anthony cried. One of the soldiers spat in his face, while the other nearly pulled his ear off as he forced the priest out of the sanctuary.

"Silence!" shouted Captain Chen. "I don't need your god to forgive me! Take him out of here at once!"

The people in the church were not sure what was happening. Many wondered if the soldiers would shoot their priest right then and there.

Then, nodding at the soldiers who raised their guns at the people, the captain added, "Leave this building at once and never return. We will put it to much better use. Perhaps it is fit to store grain or house farm animals. Now, go!"

MaMa quickly grabbed Ling's hand and followed her family and the other parishioners out. As the family started to walk home, NaiNai realized she had dropped her rosary in the church. *I can get it*, thought Pei. She stopped, but her family kept walking. Quickly, before anyone in her family noticed her missing, Pei ran back to the church.

Pei silently snuck in unnoticed by the captain and the other soldiers. She went to the back pew where her grandmother had been seated and hid. Pei could hear everything the Communists were saying.

"If their god is real then he must be tiny to live behind that little door," sneered Captain Chen as he flung open the tabernacle door. "Let's see if their god defends himself!"

With hatred raging in his eyes, the officer turned and fired his pistol into the tabernacle again and again. The sound was deafening. The golden ciborium clattered out and landed on the floor. All the consecrated Hosts spilled out.

O Jesus! They've thrown you on the floor like garbage! Pei thought, trembling with fear.

"Men, step on those little white things; this god of theirs has no power." With that, the soldiers began to stomp on the Hosts, laughing.

How can they do that to you, Jesus? Don't they know who you are? Pei thought. In addition to being scared of what the soldiers would do to her if she were found, Pei felt a terrible sadness as she watched. From where she was hiding Pei could see the Hosts. She began to count. *One, two, three . . . thirty-two consecrated Hosts on the floor.*

"We, the soldiers of the People's Liberation Army, have all the power," the captain gloated to his men. "We don't need any gods in China."

Then the soldiers knocked over the statues of Jesus and Our Lady of Sheshan. They shot the broken pieces with their pistols. Next, they mockingly splashed the holy water on themselves and on the floor and pulled the holy water fonts from the doorways. They laughed wildly as they destroyed the baptismal font.

Pei was powerless to stop the sacrilege. Once the soldiers left the church, Pei waited until everything seemed quiet. She found NaiNai's rosary and then quickly left the building and ran all the way home.

Through the window of the room he was now being held in, Father Anthony saw his young parishioner run by. The nightmare he had feared was unfolding before him. He was now a prisoner in his own home, shoved into a musty storage room. It was damp and dirty there, with the sounds of mice and rats scurrying about and cobwebs hanging everywhere. He shuddered when the filmy things touched his face.

Father Anthony was left alone, with no one to see or speak to. That night, he was given a small bowl of rice and a cup of water, so it seemed they meant for him to live. No one knew for how long, though, or what other plans the captain had for him. Fortunately, his rosary was in his pocket.

Chapter 10

A Secret Message

"MaMa, is it all right if Ling and I go to the pond?" asked Pei. "We've done all our chores and we won't stay out too long."

MaMa looked over at BaBa, who was sitting at the table. The silence stretched so long that Pei wondered if her mother had even heard her question. Pei decided to ask again. "MaMa—"

"No, Pei," MaMa interrupted sharply. "Not today; it's not safe for us to be out and about."

"But, MaMa, we'll be careful," Ling whined.

"Girls, listen to your mother," BaBa interjected.

"Yes, BaBa," Ling said sadly.

Turning to her little sister, Pei said, "Maybe we can go another time, Ling."

"You understand, Pei, I am sure. It's just too risky," BaBa explained, continuing in a low voice. "The Communists know we are Catholic. Captain Chen has already hurt you once, and we don't want that to happen again. From now on you and your brother will go to school and then come straight home."

Pei nodded. She wanted to go outside, but she understood why her parents were concerned.

Since the desecration of the church, the Catholic villagers no longer felt safe. Their non-Catholic neighbors kept their distance. No one was sure who could be trusted. There was tension throughout the village.

That afternoon, a stranger arrived in the town square. No one greeted him for fear of angering the Communist soldiers guarding the square. The stranger pushed a cart with small trinkets, some crockery, pots, and packets of tea. From her doorway, Pei could see him propping up his cart under the willow tree. She noticed that many of her neighbors also watched from the safety of their homes. *Who is he and why did he come?* wondered Pei.

The peddler soon began to play an *erhu* (arewho), a two-stringed instrument. After a while, people slowly ventured out to listen to the hauntingly beautiful music and see what else he would do. Pei, however, didn't even ask if she could join them. She knew her parents wouldn't allow it and she could enjoy the music from her door.

Once a small crowd gathered, the peddler stopped playing and began to sell his wares.

"Smell this lovely aromatic jasmine tea!" cried the peddler. "And I have brightly colored thread, too!" He held his wares out to the people with a grin.

"Who would like to try on this bracelet? My prices are the best! I also have yarn, spices, and food items for very little money!"

The peddler smiled broadly as he wrapped the peoples' purchases in paper and string. He was dressed poorly, but something about the way he spoke made him seem well-educated.

Once the crowd dispersed, the soldiers also lost interest. The peddler then wandered from street to street, offering his wares to those who did not have the courage to come out of their homes. Finally, he came to Pei's house and greeted BaBa, who was working outside.

"I won't be buying anything today, friend," BaBa said politely.

"I'm done selling for the day, sir," the peddler responded, as he leaned his cart against the corner of the house.

"Then, how can I help you?" BaBa asked him guardedly.

"I see you wear a cross," the peddler softly observed.

"Yes, what of it?" BaBa asked, a little frightened as he quickly tucked the cross under his tunic.

"I'm a priest," the peddler whispered. "Can we talk inside?"

"I don't know you. How can I know you're not lying to me?" BaBa said.

Then the peddler began to recite the Apostles' Creed in Latin, "*Credo in unum Deum . . .*"

"Okay, I believe you. Now please don't say anything else before someone overhears you and reports you to the soldiers," BaBa whispered, as he glanced from side to side. "Come in, my wife will make us some tea."

Once inside, BaBa turned to Min and said, "Move the cart to the back of our house. Pei, go and help him."

MaMa brought tea and served the priest, BaBa, and YeYe. Then she sat by the fire to mend some clothing.

"Thank you for letting me into your home and for the tea. My name is Father Chang and I came to bring a message to Father Anthony. It's from Father Kung; he's an advisor to the Bishop of Shanghai."

"I'm sorry, Father Chang, but that's impossible. Father Anthony was arrested and is being held prisoner in his house. Communist soldiers guard him day and night—no one can see him."

"When did this happen?" asked the priest.

"The Communists came to the village about a month ago," BaBa answered. "They took a religious sister and the village teacher, who is also Catholic, away in a truck and sent them to work camps. They also closed our church shortly after Christmas and have been holding Father Anthony captive."

"Nothing has been the same ever since," added YeYe sadly.

"Then the message isn't important. It's already too late," Father Chang said.

BaBa leaned forward and asked quietly, "What will happen to him?"

"Since he is a foreigner," the priest responded, "he will most likely be expelled from the country."

That night, Father Chang stayed in the family's house and celebrated Mass. The family was careful to make sure that the windows were covered with thick cloth to muffle any sound. Still, everyone spoke in a whisper. *Mass at home!* Pei thought. *They closed the church, but they can't stop you from coming to us, Jesus. Thank you,* Pei prayed.

After their dinner of rice and cabbage, Pei approached the priest.

"May I speak with you, Father Chang?"

"Yes, of course. How can I help you?"

"When I received Jesus in Holy Communion at Mass tonight I was so happy! Before the soldiers damaged the church and shut it, I had always gone to God's house to receive the Eucharist. But today, Jesus came to *my* house."

"Perhaps Jesus wanted to comfort you, Pei, and let you know how much he loves you and that he is still with you."

"But I wish that I could do the same for him. Father Chang, there are thirty-two Hosts on the floor of the church. I counted them." Pei began to wipe her eyes. "Jesus is present in those Hosts, but the soldiers dishonored him and left him there trampled on the ground. Thinking about it makes me want to go to him."

"Maybe someday, but not now," Father Chang cautioned. "Jesus understands, Pei. He knows what's in your heart."

"But I think I could find a way into the church, Father."

The priest looked sternly at Pei. "No," he said. "I know you mean well, but the church is no place for you or anyone else now. It's too dangerous."

∽∞∾

Early the next morning, the priest was on his way, dragging his cart to the next village. As she waved at Father Chang, Pei yawned. She had spent much of the night thinking about the church and the thirty-two Hosts on the floor. *I know it's dangerous, Jesus,* she prayed, *but someone has to do something.*

Chapter 11

The New Year

Despite the spirit of fear and intimidation that ruled in the village, everyone was excited about the New Year celebrations, especially the children. There would be treats, gifts, red envelopes with small sums of money, and perhaps even some fruit.

Once the houses had been thoroughly cleaned inside and out, the New Year, 1949, the Year of the Ox, would be greeted by red lanterns. Because BaBa had owned a fabric shop, the family was lucky enough to have enough red cloth for several lanterns, which they hung on the front door and on tree limbs.

Ling said, "When can we do our paper cutting, MaMa?"

"I suppose we could start now, Ling. Pei, go get the red paper. Min, get the scissors. We can use BaBa's big cutting table and make our decorations together."

"But why do we have to make everything red?" asked Ling.

"Because it's a tradition and red is the color of good luck!" MaMa replied.

The red paper was spread out on the large table, and the family went to work cutting out designs of pine trees and ducks to decorate their doors and windows.

"Min can put them up. That will be his job," said BaBa.

∞

On New Year's Eve morning MaMa was already up, making preparations for her special dinner that evening. She was preparing traditional foods, with Pei's help and NaiNai's supervision. There would be dumplings and rice balls and *nian gao* (nyen gaow) cake. This year, though, servings would be small, and there would be no pork.

Before long, the water was boiling.

"I love making dumplings," said NaiNai with a faraway look in her eyes. "It reminds me of when

I was young. I must have made thousands of them in my lifetime!"

"Let's sing the song I taught you last year," Pei said. "Do you remember it?"

"No," said Ling.

"Well, I'll sing it for you and then you can chime in, all right?"

Whirring, whirring snowflakes fall.
Crack, crack! Set off the firecrackers.
Clang, boom, boom! Clang, boom, boom!
Play with the dragon lanterns.
Haha! Haha! New Year is coming.

For the rest of the day, parts of that little song could be heard drifting through the house and outdoors. It had been a long time since anyone had relaxed enough to have fun. But Pei's mind returned to the church from time to time.

"Pei?" BaBa called from the dinner table, interrupting her thoughts. "We're all waiting for you!"

Pei's cheeks flushed with embarrassment as she joined the others.

"Let's stand now and hold hands as we ask for God's blessings: Tonight, on the eve of a New Year, we thank you, Lord, for your many gifts to us. We ask you to protect our family and our village from all evil. Help us to trust in your loving care, even in these dark times. Amen."

After the dinner had been eaten, the children received their gifts. NaiNai and YeYe greeted each child with the customary "Blessings, happiness, and prosperity" before handing out a red envelope with a small amount of money in it. Then MaMa and BaBa gave them the gifts they had made.

For Min, BaBa had redesigned an old coat of fine gray wool. "Let me see you in it, my son," BaBa said, as he turned his son around. "You are almost a man! Soon, you'll be taller than I am."

"Look how well it fits you!" MaMa exclaimed. She had sewn a bit of black embroidery on the collar, so that Min would remember it was specially made for him.

"Thank you, BaBa. Thank you, MaMa. This is so special, and it's warm, too."

"What about *me*?" Ling asked expectantly.

"We could never forget about you, little one. We have something special for you, too. Here, open it!" MaMa handed Ling a bag. Inside was a beautiful, red velvet vest and matching hat, both embroidered with roses.

"Oh, MaMa, BaBa!" she cried. "It's so beautiful. And it's *mine*!"

Finally it was Pei's turn. She was excited to see what her parents had made for her. She knew they must have saved scraps of cloth from the shop to make these gifts, even though they hardly received any business these days.

"And this is for you, Pei," MaMa said. "I hope you like it."

Pei found herself staring—speechless—at a beautiful pink jacket her parents had made.

"It's so lovely!" Pei said with excitement. "The pink silk is so soft, and the embroidery! MaMa, these birds look like they're flying, and I can almost smell the flowers! And BaBa, it fits perfectly. The sleeves are just where they should be."

"How lucky that rich lady didn't need all the silk she ordered!" said NaiNai.

"Thank you both so much. I love it! " Pei said.

Soon after, the family joined their neighbors who were outdoors lighting firecrackers and enjoying the loud bangs and shrieks of laughter that echoed through the little village.

"Where did you get that jacket?" Jiang-Mei asked Pei.

"My parents made it from some scraps in their shop. Isn't it beautiful?" Pei exclaimed.

"It is," Jiang-Mei agreed wistfully. "I wish my parents could make me something like that."

Pei noticed that a few of the Communist soldiers had joined the festivities. The sight of them reminded Pei of the abandoned Hosts on the floor of the church.

Chapter 12

A Risky Adventure

At first, Father Anthony thought he was seeing things. From the small room where he was kept prisoner, the priest saw a flash of pink through a gap in the boarded-up window. Wondering who would be walking near the church in the middle of the night, Father Anthony held his breath and listened. The sound of light footsteps was barely audible to him. The priest prayed that no one else could hear it. If whoever was outside was caught, that person—and probably that person's family—would be severely punished.

∞

Unable to sleep that night, Pei had decided to risk sneaking into the church. She held her breath as she crept past the rectory window. Pei peeked around the corner of the rectory and saw a Communist soldier leaning against the rectory door. He had fallen asleep. *A few more steps and I'll be there*, she thought. Pei hoped that she would be able to enter through the back door of the church. But when she finally got there, she saw that it had been boarded up. A big sign with Chinese characters warned, "NO TRESPASSING." Pei took a deep breath as she tried to think of another way in.

Just then, Pei noticed a broken window on the side of the church. *I think I can get in there*, she thought. She walked over to the window and rose on her toes to peer in. Pei saw that a bench had been pushed up against the other side of the window. *If I can climb onto the window ledge, I should be able to reach that bench. But I'll have to be careful not to cut myself.*

Making the Sign of the Cross, Pei prayed silently, *I know my parents would be upset if they knew I was here. But I have to be here with you, Jesus. Please don't let the guard wake up, and help me get inside.*

Stepping on an overturned pail, Pei pulled herself up and over the ledge. She crouched on the bench and waited until her eyes adjusted to the darkness inside. Pei's heart was pounding and she could hear herself breathe. Once her breathing became quieter, she took a look around.

Bullet holes riddled the sanctuary walls and floors. Echoes of gunfire and the fear she'd felt the last time she had been in the church returned to her. Pei trembled and sank to the floor, aware that any noise she made might attract a soldier's attention. She lifted her head and saw the altar. Crawling toward the front of the church as quietly as possible, Pei avoided the sharp fragments of the broken statues that littered her path.

What is that? wondered Pei as she noticed an odd shape lying to her left. Drawing closer, she picked it up to examine it. It was part of a hand from one of the statues—a hand with a red indentation in its palm. *It's Jesus' hand!* Pei realized. *I don't understand it!* Her muscles became tense as she felt a flash of anger. *How could they do that to you, Jesus?*

Pei wished she could put all the pieces of the statues back together. But she knew it wasn't possible. Trying to calm herself, she reasoned, *This hand isn't real; it's only a part of a statue. Jesus is truly here, present in the Hosts scattered on the floor. That is why I'm here.* Pei made her way up to the altar and behind it. There, on the floor, were the consecrated Hosts—all thirty-two of them.

Pei was sad to see the dirty marks of soldiers' boots on the Hosts. She bowed down in adoration. Pei knew that Jesus—the *real* Jesus—was truly present.

What do I do? Pei wondered. *I wish I could receive them all right now. But at Mass I receive only one Host. That's what I'll do now. And I'll just have to keep coming back.* Taking one of the Hosts on her tongue and consuming it, she felt grateful that she was able to receive Holy Communion again. Then Pei began to pray silently.

Jesus, I've missed coming to this church. I've missed spending time with you in adoration. And I'm sorry that the Communist soldiers threw you on the ground and then stepped on you. Please forgive them.

So much has changed. They took Sister Elizabeth and Sifu Yang away, and Father Anthony is a prisoner in his own home. MaMa and BaBa are worried, and they won't let me and Min and Ling play with our neighbors. And I can hear NaiNai praying the Rosary at night asking Our Lady of Sheshan to help us. Jesus, please keep me and my family safe. Please protect Sister Elizabeth, Sifu Yang, Father Anthony, and Father Chang . . .

Pei held nothing back. She shared everything with Jesus. Suddenly, she realized that she had no idea how much time had passed. *I must have been here for over an hour. I've got to get home before anyone notices I'm gone,* Pei thought. She crawled back to the broken window as quickly and as quietly as possible. Just as Pei was about to lift herself onto the windowsill, she turned toward the altar. *Good night, Jesus. I promise I'll come back for another visit tomorrow.*

Chapter 13

The Pink Jacket

Every night Pei returned to the church to consume one more Host and spend an hour or more in prayer and adoration. Her days, filled with school and chores, were similar to what they had been before the Communists had arrived. But it was still difficult to accept the change at her school. Teacher Yang had been a kind, loving teacher. Comrade Zhao was harsh and did not seem to care as much for her students' well-being. All she seemed to care about was passing down the philosophy of Communism. Every day Pei and her classmates were required to fill their notebooks with more of Chairman Mao Zedong's words and Communist slogans. Comrade Zhao would often play favorites and pit the students against each other. Classroom competitions were anything but friendly.

One day, Comrade Zhao lined the students up against the wall of the room.

"Today we are going to play a little game," she explained. "Children who answer correctly will receive a treat. Those who do not will do without it." Pei noticed a basket of fruit on the desk.

"First question: Who are we?"

The first hand shot up. Once called on, a small boy confidently answered, "We are all good Communists, Comrade."

"Excellent!" she replied, handing him a piece of fruit. "Remember that we are all workers, and no one is above anyone else."

Jiang-Mei, Pei's best friend, raised her hand.

"What is it, Jiang-Mei?" Comrade Zhao impatiently demanded.

Jiang-Mei frowned at Pei, then asked, "If no one is better than anyone else, then why is it that *some* of us have better things?"

"Explain," the teacher continued.

"Well," the girl said bitterly, "Pei has a lovely new jacket and I don't."

Pei could feel her face go hot. She never thought her best friend would turn on her like that. She had no idea that Jiang-Mei was so jealous of her. Pei nervously ran her fingers over her mother's beautiful needlework.

"But it's mine!" Pei cried. "BaBa made it for me and MaMa embroidered it!"

"Quiet!" Comrade Zhao shouted. "Jiang-Mei is correct. In the new China, everything belongs to the people. Why should you and you alone have that jacket?" All eyes were fixed on Comrade Zhao as she paced the front of the room. "You are no better than any of your fellow classmates. Now take that jacket off immediately and give it to its co-owner, Jiang-Mei. You will wear her jacket from now on."

"That's not fair; her jacket is old and ugly!" mumbled Pei.

"I will have no backtalk from you!" shouted the teacher. "Give her the jacket at once!"

Slowly, Pei removed her jacket and handed it over to Jiang-Mei. Its new owner put on the jacket, smiled smugly, and sat down. Tears tumbled onto Pei's cheeks as she put on the old brown jacket and took her place. For the rest of the day, Pei was distracted with anger and worry. *I don't understand how Jiang-Mei could do this to me. I knew she loved my jacket, and I would have let her borrow it if she had asked! How am I going to explain this when I get home? What am I going to do? BaBa and MaMa will be so angry with me.* She couldn't think about anything else.

When Pei came home that afternoon, MaMa asked, "What are you wearing?"

Hanging her head, Pei realized she would have to answer.

"Where did it come from?" MaMa continued. "And where is your pink jacket?"

"Jiang-Mei wanted my new jacket, and the teacher said I had to give it to her," Pei said, wiping away a tear.

"I don't understand, Pei. Jiang-Mei is your best friend. And BaBa and I made that jacket just for you."

"Comrade Zhao said that good Communists share everything they have. Sharing is good and I like to share, but that jacket was mine! Jiang-Mei didn't even ask if she could borrow it. I didn't have any choice. The jacket now belongs to Jiang-Mei. It isn't mine anymore."

"Oh Pei, I'm so sorry that the jacket we made for you brought you so much grief," MaMa said, holding Pei close. "I'll tell your father what happened."

∞

Pei went to bed and waited for everyone to fall asleep. As she lay there, Pei thought about the beautiful pink jacket. BaBa had saved such a fine piece of pink silk, a remnant from a wealthy woman's robe, for her new jacket. It was so lovely and BaBa rarely worked in fine fabrics anymore.

Pei thought of how BaBa always told the family that God is trustworthy, that he is always there when we need him.

But where was God when I needed him today? Pei thought angrily. She could feel her anger flare. *Why did God allow Jiang-Mei to take my jacket?*

Pei was tired and not certain that she even wanted to go back to the church again. Still, she wanted answers. Without a sound, Pei grabbed Jiang-Mei's old coat and stole into the night.

Chapter 14

A Near Escape

The peace and comfort Pei had always felt inside the church wasn't there. From the floor just inside the broken window, Pei's hurt welled up and overwhelmed her. Tears streamed down her cheeks in silence.

Why, Jesus, why? Why did you let Jiang-Mei take my jacket? Why would my best friend hurt me like that? How could you let this happen? Pei had never prayed that way before. She hurled all her questions at God at once. If she had been able to speak aloud, Pei would have been out of breath. *I've been coming here every night, sneaking past the guard, crawling through the window. Doesn't that count?*

Hunched on the floor in the dark and drafty church, Pei felt very much alone. *So many*

questions, she thought, *and no answers.* She heard
a rustling sound outside, probably the restless
guard sleeping against the door. Suddenly, other
thoughts flooded her mind. An unfamiliar voice
spoke in her head.

*Why are you here, Pei? There is no one in this
empty building. You're a fool!*

Startled, Pei sat up straight and shook her
head.

The voice continued, *For the past two weeks
you've been coming here and risking your life for
nothing!*

Nothing? No! Pei thought. *I know why I've been
coming—*

*What about your friend Jiang-Mei? She doesn't
even care about you. And what about your pink
jacket, Pei?* the voice taunted. *Why didn't God help
you?* Her heart pounded in the silence. *I'll tell you
why . . . because God isn't real.*

Pei gasped. *Jesus!* she prayed, *help me not to
listen to these lies. I know you're real. You could have
done something to stop Jiang-Mei. Why didn't you?*
Pei's fists tightened and her body began to shake.
Why?

Pei poured out every drop of her anger before
God until none was left. Gazing ahead into the
darkness, her eyes settled on one of the broken

statue pieces scattered on the floor. She could make out flames and a crown of thorns. It was the Sacred Heart of Jesus. *Where are you, God?* She breathed deeply. Only silence remained, and in that silence Pei heard another and more gentle voice.

Pei, I am here.

She crawled forward toward the altar, embarrassed that she had forgotten the abandoned Hosts. *I'm sorry, Jesus. I believe you are with me*, Pei prayed. She took one of the fifteen remaining Hosts and ate it. The peace she sought had returned. *I trust you, Lord.*

Pei realized she might never get her pink jacket back. But she also knew that she had Jesus, and that he would never leave her. Ready to return home, Pei tiptoed to the broken window and quietly climbed over the sill.

The night was cloudless and full of stars. The moon was high in the sky. Pei smiled. Walking in the shadows of the trees along the dirt road, Pei wondered how long she had been inside the church. So much had happened there. Now, all she could think about was getting back into her bed without waking her parents and grandparents.

"We never see anyone at this hour," a man's voice said.

"I don't know why we have to walk this boring village at night. Nothing happens," responded another man.

Pei realized that they must be soldiers. They sounded close, and Pei knew she needed to hide. As she dashed behind a bush, Pei kicked up a few pebbles with one of her shoes.

"Who's there?" one of the Communist soldiers demanded.

Pei covered her mouth with her hands, afraid that even her breathing could betray her.

"Shine the flashlight there, by those bushes," the other added.

The beam of light swept across the bush near where Pei was hiding.

Help me, Jesus, please hide me! Pei prayed desperately.

"There's no one there. It must have been an animal. Let's move on," the first soldier said.

The soldiers began to walk away. Pei waited until she could no longer hear the sound of their steps before she crept out from behind the bush. Her heart was pounding and she could feel her whole body trembling, but she moved as quickly as she could.

Inside the safety of her home, Pei hung Jiang-Mei's old brown jacket near the door. Suddenly, it hit her. She could have been caught tonight. *If I had been wearing my pink jacket, the soldiers would have seen me! If only I could have trusted that God can bring good from anything. Thank you, God, for saving me!*

Chapter 15

Trouble at School

"This is the third time, Pei," Mother said with frustration. "You need to get up for school *now*. You're not sick, and if you're late who knows what Comrade Zhao will do!"

Bleary-eyed, Pei got dressed and ate breakfast. She ran out the door wearing the brown jacket and hurried to school.

Throughout the day Pei struggled to concentrate. She was so exhausted from her late-night visits to the church and early rising for school. Nothing Comrade Zhao taught pierced the fog of Pei's drowsiness. She felt herself nodding off.

"I asked you a question, Pei," Comrade Zhao barked. "Your classmates are waiting for the answer."

Jolting up from drowsy sleep and feeling ashamed, Pei replied in a quiet voice, "I'm sorry, Comrade, I didn't hear the question."

Comrade Zhao slammed her fist on the table. "China's future is for workers—not for sleepers! There is no place for daydreaming or laziness. Stand up!"

Pei stood on trembling legs. Looking up, she confirmed what she dreaded—*everyone* was staring at her. Then Comrade Zhao told her to sit at the front of the room and face the class. She forced Pei to wear a sign that said "stupid and lazy." Pei could hardly hold back her tears.

When Comrade Zhao told the class it was time for lunch, Pei got up from her seat at the front of the class. She was about to remove the sign she had been wearing.

"What do you think you're doing, dog?" her teacher demanded. "Your punishment isn't over. You will wear that sign for the rest of the day. And before you eat your lunch, *you* will fetch the water for everyone else."

"Yes, Comrade," Pei answered.

Picking up the two wooden buckets by the door, Pei left the classroom and went to the well outside. Pei quickly pumped water into the buckets. *What's going to happen to me when my parents hear about all this? Will they find out about my late-night visits that are making me so sleepy?* Pei wondered. *I have to talk to Min.*

Grabbing a handle in each of her hands, Pei tried to lift the buckets from the ground. *These buckets are so heavy. I'll have to carry them one at a time—which means I'll run out of time to eat lunch. Comrade Zhao won't give me extra time . . . will this day ever end? Jesus, help me.*

At long last, the teacher dismissed the children for the day. Pei returned the sign and put on her jacket. Waiting just outside the building was her brother, Min.

"Are you all right, Pei?" asked Min with concern as they walked home. "You brought dishonor to our family today. Falling asleep in class isn't like you. Is this about losing your pink jacket?"

"No, I don't care about it so much anymore," Pei said.

"Then what's going on?" Min questioned.

Pei stopped for a moment. She wanted to tell him everything—about the sleeping guards, her visits to the church, consuming the Hosts, and almost being caught. But that would put Min in danger. "I can't tell you," she answered, looking directly into his eyes. "Min, please don't tell MaMa and BaBa what happened at school today. Please."

"I may not have to," Min said as they neared home. "Look who's standing at the door."

"How did *she* get here so fast?" Pei said quietly. Comrade Zhao glared at Min and Pei as she pivoted to leave.

"Maybe the Communists have wings!" he replied in an amused whisper. For the first time that day, Pei smiled.

As they reached the door, Ling came running out. "Guess who was just here?" she asked. Without waiting for Min or Pei to respond, Ling continued, "Your teacher wanted to speak with MaMa and BaBa about you, Pei." Ling spun around chanting, "Pei's in trouble. Pei's in trouble."

Pei's shoulders drooped. "Ling, what did she tell them?"

Coming to a stop, Ling looked at her sister. "Nothing; they're not home. NaiNai and YeYe sent me outside and they talked to her."

Pei felt relieved, at least for the moment. She went inside to begin her chores. As Pei swept the floor, she tried to let go of the day's humiliation. *This all happened because I fell asleep in class*, Pei thought as she worked. *I wouldn't have fallen asleep if I wasn't staying up late so I can go to the church and visit Jesus. I'm just so tired all the time. Maybe I need to stop . . .*

Pei's thoughts were interrupted by someone calling her name. "Pei," repeated NaiNai, "come and speak with me."

Turning toward her grandmother, Pei asked, "What is it, NaiNai?"

"You know that your *sifu* was here a little while ago," NaiNai responded. "She told us that you weren't paying attention in class. Is that true?"

"I wasn't daydreaming, NaiNai," Pei replied sheepishly. "I couldn't stay awake because I was so tired."

NaiNai looked at Pei and the dark circles under her eyes. "Are you having trouble sleeping at night?"

Pei didn't want to tell her grandmother about her visits, but she also knew it was wrong to lie. "Yes, NaiNai, I don't fall asleep right away and the morning comes too fast."

"Then, why don't you take a nap now before dinner?" NaiNai suggested. "I'll help with the laundry."

Pei threw her arms around NaiNai and hugged her. Then she whispered, "Are you going to tell MaMa and BaBa?"

"Not this time," her grandmother assured Pei. "But don't let it happen again. Maybe you should think about going to bed earlier."

✁

When Pei woke up from her nap, MaMa and BaBa were home and MaMa was helping NaiNai prepare supper. She was relieved when her parents did not ask her why she had been sleeping. Everyone had many things on their minds.

After supper, as the family prepared to pray the Rosary, YeYe asked, "Has there been any news about Father Anthony?"

"I'm afraid not," said BaBa. "Nobody has seen him. In fact, I wonder if he's still being held in his house."

Min interjected, "I thought they were going to send him away."

"But no one has seen him leave," said MaMa. "And there's still an armed guard outside the door; he must still be there. I wish there was a way we could know that he is all right."

"All we can do is pray. Let's remember Father Anthony, Sister Elizabeth, *Sifu* Yang, and Father Chang in this Rosary. We'll ask Our Lady of Sheshan to keep them safe."

Later that evening Pei lay in bed. Her grandmother kept her word and said nothing to Pei's parents. *Hopefully YeYe won't say anything either,* she thought. *This has been such a horrible day. Maybe I shouldn't go to the church tonight. I could skip one night, couldn't I?* Pei fell asleep before she could think it through. A few hours later, Pei's eyes snapped open. Everyone else in the house was asleep.

Maybe I will go to the church after all, Pei decided as she rolled out of bed.

Chapter 16

A Change of Heart

After tonight, there will only be seven Hosts left on the floor, Pei thought as she walked along the dusty road, her head down, thinking. Min had run after school to help BaBa, and Pei's mind was full of thoughts. It had been another difficult day.

A classmate had tripped and spilled the whole bucket of water he'd been carrying to the classroom. Comrade Zhao had hit him on the shoulders with her ruler and had forced him to sit with the same humiliating sign Pei had worn around her neck. Pei had known how bad he felt and smiled at him whenever she'd caught his eye. He had looked so miserable the entire afternoon. It seemed like Comrade Zhao punished someone every day.

Since that day a week earlier, Pei had managed to stay awake and out of trouble at school. Still, she didn't enjoy school the way she used to when *Sifu* Yang had taught them. *Where are Sifu Yang and Sister Elizabeth?* Pei wondered. *Oh, Jesus, wherever they are, please help them,* she prayed.

Suddenly, Pei came to a stop when she realized that someone was blocking her path. The first thing she noticed as she raised her head was a hand holding a beautifully embroidered, pink jacket. Pei inhaled deeply, then looked at Jiang-Mei.

She was wearing an old, brown jacket, probably her brother's.

"Hello, Pei," Jiang-Mei said, scuffling her shoes in the dirt.

"Hello," Pei responded, not knowing what else to say.

"I've wanted to talk to you," Jiang-Mei continued. "I . . . I just don't know how to begin."

Although Jiang-Mei appeared to be sincere, Pei was hesitant to trust her. "What do you want? I don't have anything else for you to take from me."

Tears filled the young girl's eyes. "No, Pei, I don't want to take anything from anyone. I'm so sorry for what I did to you."

"You're sorry? Why should I believe you?" Pei countered.

"I understand," Jiang-Mei offered sadly. "If I were you I wouldn't believe me either. But I've been thinking a lot about what I did—and I'm so ashamed."

"Then why did you do it?" Pei asked, her heart beginning to soften.

"I don't really have a good reason; I just wanted your jacket so much."

"But it was *my* jacket. My parents made it for *me*," Pei said, her anger rising again. "And do you know what hurt most of all? It was that I never expected my best friend to take it from me. It was like losing you and my jacket on the same day!"

"I really *am* sorry, Pei. I've been thinking of everything Sister Elizabeth taught us, and I know what I did was wrong. I was just so envious that I didn't care about anything except getting your jacket. I want to give it back to you now. Maybe someday you can forgive me."

"I don't know, Jiang-Mei," Pei said, shrugging her shoulders. Jiang-Mei carefully handed her the jacket, and turned to walk away.

"I'll try," said Pei, too softly to be heard.

∞

The next morning, Pei felt hopeful. The night before she had visited Jesus in the church and asked him to help her to forgive Jiang-Mei. Jesus had helped her to let go of her anger, and now Pei felt like she could forgive her friend. *Thank you for helping me last night, Jesus. I think I can forgive Jiang-Mei now*, Pei thought as she prepared for school. Deciding it was best if Comrade Zhao didn't know that Jiang-Mei had returned the jacket, she left it at home and went to school.

Pei walked up the path and knocked on the door of a house nearby. She could hear someone approaching. The door opened slowly.

"Good morning, Jiang-Mei," Pei said smiling. "Would you like to walk to school with me today?"

Jiang-Mei's face lit up. "Oh, Pei! Of course I would!"

The two girls walked side by side, not saying much at first. But by the time they were half-way to school, Pei and Jiang-Mei were talking and laughing. Pei was happy to have a best friend again.

As they passed the church, Jiang-Mei wondered aloud, "Do you ever think about Father Anthony, Sister Elizabeth, or *Sifu* Yang?"

"I think about them all the time; I wonder how they are," Pei replied.

"No one knows," Jiang-Mei said. "I just hope they're giving Father Anthony enough food and water. I miss the way things used to be."

"I do too," Pei agreed, yawning. "The Communists have changed everything."

"Pei," Jiang-Mei asked, "why are you so tired all the time?"

Just as Pei was trying to figure out what to say, Comrade Zhao stood at the door and rang the bell. *At least I don't have to answer her question now,* thought Pei. All the children entered the building in silence, hung up their jackets, and stood at their places. Comrade Zhao had written today's Chairman Mao quote on the blackboard. Class began.

I hope Jiang-Mei doesn't ask me about being tired again, Pei worried. *Jesus, what do I tell her if she does?*

Chapter 17

A Secret Is Revealed

At dinner that evening the family's conversation turned to Father Anthony. Ever since Father Chang's visit, the whole family had kept the two priests in their prayers.

"I heard some news today about our priest. I just don't know whether or not to believe it," BaBa said, a frown wrinkling his face.

"What did you hear?" MaMa asked.

"It seems like they'll be taking him away from the village soon," BaBa continued. "I just hope they send him back to the United States and don't kill him."

"Maybe he's already dead," said YeYe. "Who knows how they've been treating him?"

"How can we help him?" Pei asked. "Is there some way we can let Father Anthony know we're thinking of him?"

"We pass by the church and his house every day on our way to school," offered Min. "The guards are always there, but maybe we could get a message to him."

"But early in the morning there's only one guard. And he's young. He's not much older than Min," Pei added.

"That's true!" said Min with excitement. "We could be friendly to the guard and get him to tell us about Father Anthony."

"Absolutely not!" BaBa ordered. "It's too dangerous; the guard would know you were fishing for information. Then we would *all* be arrested and sent to a labor camp."

The conversation ended. A feeling of heaviness lingered in the room. The meal ended in silence.

There must be another way, Pei thought as she cleared the table.

Later that night, Pei knelt by the ruined altar. She wondered how Father Anthony was doing and prayed for him. *Lord, that first night when I couldn't get to the door of this church because of the sleeping guard, you showed me the broken window.*

Show us how to help Father Anthony before it's too late.

∽∾∽

"What are you humming, Jiang-Mei?" Min asked as he, Jiang-Mei, and Pei walked to school.

"It's 'Row, row, row your boat,' the song Father Anthony taught us. Remember?" Jiang-Mei responded.

"Oh yes," said Pei, "I remember it now."

"Anything is better than the songs Comrade Zhao is making us learn. They're all about the Communist Revolution and Chairman Mao," Min added.

The three children continued on their way to school humming together. As they passed the Communist soldier guarding the door of Father Anthony's house, their humming grew quieter. Then from inside the house they heard a voice they hadn't heard for some time. Pei's eyes grew wide. It was Father Anthony, and he was singing!

The soldier rapped on the window with the butt of his rifle.

"Quiet!" he ordered angrily. "Or I'll come in there and stop you myself!"

The children hurried past the house before the soldier could threaten them as well. *Father*

Anthony heard us and sang back! He's still alive! Thank you, Jesus! Pei prayed. *Thank you for helping us find out about him.*

∽✇∾

After school that afternoon, Jiang-Mei and Pei watched as Min ran ahead to help BaBa. "I couldn't stop thinking about Father Anthony today," said Jiang-Mei, looking around to make sure no one overheard them.

"Me, too," admitted Pei. "When I heard him singing back to us . . . I have never been so happy to hear someone!"

"I'm glad that the soldier didn't do anything to us! I got scared when he raised his rifle," Jiang-Mei said with a shudder. Noticing that her friend didn't have much of a reaction, she added, "Weren't you scared?"

"Not anymore," Pei blurted without thinking. Closing her eyes, she slapped her hand over her mouth.

Jiang-Mei came to a complete stop. Turning to look at her companion, she asked, "What's *that* supposed to mean?"

Pei uncovered her mouth and slowly opened her eyes. She scrambled for a response.

"Come on, Pei," Jiang-Mei pleaded. "I thought you trusted me again."

Pei saw the concern on her friend's face. *I do trust her,* Pei thought. *And it would be good to have someone to talk to . . .* "I do trust you," Pei started to explain. "It's just that I haven't told *anyone* about this."

"I promise I won't tell," assured Jiang-Mei.

"I know . . . but not here." Pei started to walk again and Jiang-Mei followed. The girls stepped into the nearby woods. Once Pei was sure that no one else was around to overhear them, she found an old tree stump and invited Jiang-Mei to sit down.

"So, tell me what's going on?" insisted a curious Jiang-Mei.

Pei reminded her friend of what the Communist soldiers had done on the day they arrested Father Anthony.

"I know all that already. I was there, remember?" Jiang-Mei retorted. "It's the last time we attended Mass . . . the last time we were in our beautiful little church," she added sadly.

"It's the last time *you* were in the church," Pei quietly corrected. "But *I've* been back at the church every night for almost a month." Hearing Jiang-Mei gasp, she continued, "It might sound crazy, Jiang-Mei, but I just couldn't stop thinking about the Blessed Sacrament still scattered all over the floor."

Jiang-Mei was stunned as Pei revealed how she had been sneaking into the church every night to pray an hour of adoration and consume one of the consecrated Hosts.

"I can't believe you've gotten away with it for this long," Jiang-Mei remarked once Pei had finished telling her everything. "Aren't you afraid? The soldiers will hurt you if you get caught."

"At first I was scared, and once I almost *was* caught. I know I could end up being taken away like Sister Elizabeth and *Sifu* Yang, or maybe even worse. I don't want to risk my life, but, like I said, they threw Jesus on the floor. They even stomped on him with their boots! I just *had* to do something. And you know what, Jiang-Mei?"

"What, Pei?" her friend asked, shaking her head.

"Spending time with Jesus in the church is the best thing I've ever done. It's so peaceful when you're with him like that," Pei said, almost smiling.

"But you can't keep going there. You've got to stop! It's too dangerous," Jiang-Mei insisted. "Pei, they'll kill you!" she warned.

"I'm really careful. I go when everyone is asleep; even the soldier on guard is asleep. Besides," Pei reasoned, "there are only two more Hosts; tomorrow night will be my last visit."

Chapter 18

The Last Visit

It was a clear and starry night with only a sliver of moon in the sky. Pei walked quietly and carefully along the abandoned street, thinking, *There are so many stars, and they're so beautiful! I remember trying to count the stars last summer when we visited NaiNai and YeYe on the farm. Maybe we can do that again this summer.* As she approached the church, she noted that the guard at the door was—as usual—asleep and snoring. His loud snores punctured the stillness of the night. Tonight, though, an empty bottle of liquor lay on its side next to him. She headed straight for the familiar broken window.

With quick and well-practiced moves, Pei entered the church. She made her way to the sanctuary on her hands and knees, feeling in the darkness for the last host on the floor. The night before, she had left the very last Host there, under the altar. When she found it, a wave of joy welled up in her heart. *One, only one left,* she thought.

Kneeling before Jesus, Pei closed her eyes and prayed. *I'm here, Jesus. But it's the last time. I don't know when I'll ever be able to pray like this or receive you again.* A tear rolled down her cheek. When she opened her eyes she took the consecrated Host and ate it. Pei bowed her head in gratitude. Pei didn't need to say anything. She sat in the dark church aware of God's presence. He was everywhere—around her and inside her. *Thank you, Jesus,* she prayed silently. *I'll miss you.*

Then in her heart Pei heard the gentle voice of God speak again. *Don't be afraid, Pei. I will always be with you. Through your Baptism, I dwell within you.* **You** *are my chapel.* At once she understood what his promise meant. She was never alone and never would be. At church, at home, in the village, at school—wherever she was, God was too. And even more, God was with Sister Elizabeth and Father Anthony. He never leaves those who believe in him.

"Wake up!" a man shouted outside.

Pei froze. The voice came from near where the guard was stationed at the door of the rectory.

Her eyes scanned the church for the darkest corner. *Stay still!* she told herself. *He will probably just move on. He probably won't come into the church.*

"Stand up, you lazy dog!" the man ordered. Pei recognized his voice. It was Captain Chen. "How can you protect the new China from its enemies when you are asleep—or drunk?" he demanded. The guard groaned as he scuffled to his feet.

"I'm sorry, sir," he said nervously.

"Just what are you guarding, this tree?" Captain Chen taunted.

"No, sir," the soldier responded, "I'm guarding the priest and this building." The soldier gestured toward the church.

"You are lucky the priest has not escaped!" yelled Captain Chen, seeing Father Anthony peering from one of the windows. "Let's see how well you have guarded this building."

I've got to hide. They're coming in! Pei thought. As she heard the chain and lock rattling at the front door, Pei darted to the wall and flattened herself against it. The door creaked open, and the two men walked toward the altar. Everything was pitch black. Pei could see nothing, and she knew the Communist soldiers couldn't see anything either. Then the guard she had evaded for all these weeks turned on his flashlight. The light swept the floor and landed on her shoes.

"Who are you?" demanded Captain Chen, grabbing the flashlight and shining it into Pei's eyes. "What did you come here to steal?"

If I tell him my name, my whole family will be sent away. Jesus, give me courage!

"Answer me!" he shouted all the louder. The guard drew his rifle and pointed it at her.

"I . . . I'm not stealing anything . . ." Pei stammered. "I just came here to be with Jesus . . . to pray."

"Pray?" Captain Chen laughed. "This kind of ignorance and superstition will be stamped out." Pei shook with fear. Turning to the guard, he continued to shout, "You fool! You let a little village girl humiliate you!"

Angry and ashamed, the drunken guard began to beat Pei with the butt of his rifle.

"Jesus!" she cried out.

Locked in the rectory, Father Anthony yelled for help. But the enraged guard hit her again and again, until Pei's lifeless body slumped onto the floor.

Wanting to show the consequences of defiance, Captain Chen fired a few shots from his pistol into the air. He knew that the villagers would gather to see what had happened. Doors opened up and down the lanes, and soon everyone was rushing toward the church. Pale and distraught, Jiang-Mei was the first to enter. Others followed quickly afterward. No one was prepared for what they saw. Everyone gasped. In front of the altar lay the body of a young girl.

MaMa reached for BaBa's hand. "Where's Pei?" she whispered.

"Let this be a warning to all of you," sneered Captain Chen.

"Pei!" MaMa screamed as she recognized that the crumpled body on the ground was her daughter's. Her scream pierced the dark night sky.

BaBa held MaMa in his arms. She looked as if she were on the brink of fainting. Tears ran silently down her cheeks.

The villagers stood in shock, their mouths hanging open. Some brushed away tears.

"Go home!" yelled Captain Chen. "Don't mourn this child. She held on to the ways of foreigners. A new age is here."

BaBa approached Captain Chen with his hands folded, quietly pleading. The Captain ignored BaBa as he picked up Pei's body and carried her home to be buried.

Epilogue

Everyone in the television studio was mesmerized by what Archbishop Sheen had said.

The interviewer took a deep breath to collect his thoughts. Taking a sip of water from a glass, he remarked, "That's quite a story."

"It's a lot more than just a story," responded Archbishop Sheen as he wiped his brow. "It's how this young girl lived and it's her legacy. I'm sure she had no idea that her love for Jesus in the Blessed Sacrament would inspire a priest on the other side of the world."

"Inspire? What do you mean?" asked the interviewer.

Archbishop Sheen leaned back in his chair and took a deep breath. "When I was ordained a priest I promised the Lord that I would spend an hour in front of the tabernacle with him every day.

"Hearing Pei's story has helped me to keep this promise. It took great courage for this child to risk her life night after night just because she loved Jesus. All I have to do is leave my room or office to go to the church to pray. On days when I am tired or think I'm too busy to pray, Pei inspires me."

"How did you hear about her?" the interviewer questioned.

"After a year of captivity," the archbishop responded, "Father Anthony was deported by the Communist government and he returned to the United States. I met him in Washington, D.C., where I was teaching. It was Father Anthony who first told me Pei's story. I was moved to tears."

The interviewer looked up and noticed one of the cameramen quickly wiping a tear away.

Archbishop Sheen continued, "Then, many years later, when I was visiting San Francisco, a Chinese woman came to see me. She said that her name was Jiang-Mei and that Father Anthony had suggested she come to meet me. Jiang-Mei was able to fill in the parts of the story that Father Anthony didn't know. She also told me that she had decided to join Pei at her last visit to the church that night. But she arrived too late. Her friend's devotion to the Blessed Sacrament inspired Jiang-Mei to make a daily hour of adoration as soon as she was able. And she wanted others to be inspired by Pei's witness. Her story about Pei is the one I just told you."

"Well, Archbishop Sheen, Pei lives on when her story is shared. I'm sure our viewers will be as inspired by her as you have been," the interviewer said. "I know I am."

Editor's Note

This fictionalized account is based on the true story of an eleven-year-old Chinese girl who risked her life to visit Jesus in the Blessed Sacrament after a tabernacle was desecrated and thirty-two Hosts fell to the ground. The young girl returned thirty-two times to consume each Host and spend time with Jesus in the Blessed Sacrament. This young girl's heroism inspired Archbishop Fulton Sheen and encouraged his love for Jesus in the Blessed Sacrament. We do not know exactly when Archbishop Sheen found out about this little girl's heroic example. We are not even sure of the little girl's name or when the incident took place. Some speculate that the young girl died during the Boxer Rebellion and inspired Fulton Sheen during his days in the seminary to begin making a daily hour of adoration. Others, including the Cardinal Kung Foundation, believe that the incident occurred at the end of the Chinese Civil War. Regardless of the exact details, we know that the incident occurred and that it inspired Fulton Sheen in his devotion to the presence of Jesus in the Blessed Sacrament. We hope this little girl's story has inspired you as well.

Discussion Questions

1. Why do you think Pei risked her life to visit Jesus in the Blessed Sacrament? Do you think she should have done what she did? If you were in Pei's place, would you risk your life to visit Jesus? Would you have done anything differently?

2. Which character in the story do you think is most like you? Was there one moment in the story that made you feel inspired? Happy? Angry?

3. How do you think Pei's family felt about her death? What do you think happened after Pei died?

4. How has this story changed the way you think about the Eucharist? How will you feel differently about the Eucharist the next time you go to Mass and receive the Blessed Sacrament? What was one thing you learned about the Eucharist from this book?

5. Pei really believed that Jesus was present in the thirty-two Hosts that were scattered on the floor. Do you believe that Jesus is present in the Blessed Sacrament? If so, what can you do to show that you believe Jesus is present in the Eucharist? If not, can you share your

doubts with someone and talk about this story with that person?

6. Do you think Jiang-Mei should have told an adult that Pei was sneaking out at night? Do you think anyone else in the story should have done anything differently?

7. What did you think of the ideas that Comrade Zhao, Captain Chen, and the rest of the Communists shared in the story? Were there some ideas you agreed with? Any you disagreed with?

8. It was dangerous to be a Catholic in China after the Communist Party took over. It still is dangerous to practice the faith in China. How do you think you would feel if you could not practice your faith freely? Is there anything you appreciate after having read this story?

9. What are some important ideas or lessons that you have learned from reading this story?

10. Why do you think Fulton Sheen was inspired by this eleven-year-old girl? Do her actions inspire you? Do you think your actions could ever inspire an adult? Have you ever done anything that an adult was proud of or happy about?

Glossary

Chairman Mao (maow): the leader of the Chinese Communist Party from 1945–1976

Comrade (KOM-rad): title used in a Communist society when addressing another person

Dim sum (dim suhm): typical Chinese cuisine prepared as small bite-sized portions of food; often includes steamed dumplings and rolls

Erhu (are-who): Chinese two-stringed instrument, sometimes called a "Chinese violin"

Nian gao (nyen gaow): a sweet, sticky cake made of rice that is traditionally eaten during the Chinese New Year

Qipao (chee-pow): one-piece Chinese dress that was popular in Shanghai beginning in the 1920s and made fashionable by socialites and upper class women

Sifu (see-foo): term of respect that can be used for a teacher

Ellen Lucey Prozeller

has been a teacher on all levels, from elementary school through college. She has also taught religious education on a volunteer basis for many years. She holds an MA in English literature and has published articles and short stories in *The New York Times*, *St. Anthony Messenger*, *America Magazine*, and more. In addition, Mrs. Prozeller has worked as an editor and corporate trainer. She is married and has two adult daughters and four grandchildren.

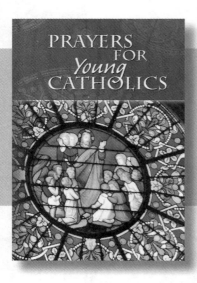

Give the
ideal gift
today!

Prayers for Young Catholics brings together
a collection of prayers—some simple, others more
advanced—accompanied by stunning artwork that
will captivate young readers.

Here you'll find:

- prayers from the Bible
- prayers to Mary and the saints
- prayers for various needs and situations

Giving it as a gift? There's a presentation page to
make it memorable. *Prayers for Young Catholics*
will help guide readers through life's ups and downs
in a book that will be treasured for years to come.

Ages 8–12.

ISBN: 0-8198-5995-8
Hardcover, 192 pages
$14.95 USD

Who are the Daughters of St. Paul?

We are Catholic sisters with a mission. Our task is to bring the love of Jesus to everyone like Saint Paul did. You can find us in over 50 countries. Our founder, Blessed James Alberione, showed us how to reach out to the world through the media. That's why we publish books, make movies and apps, record music, broadcast on radio, perform concerts, help people at our bookstores, visit parishes, host JClub book fairs, use social media and the Internet, and pray for all of you.

Visit our Website at www.pauline.org

Pauline
BOOKS & MEDIA

The Daughters of St. Paul operate book and media centers at the following addresses. Visit, call, or write the one nearest you today, or find us at www.paulinestore.org.

CALIFORNIA
3908 Sepulveda Blvd, Culver City, CA 90230   310-397-8676
3250 Middlefield Road, Menlo Park, CA 94025   650-369-4230

FLORIDA
145 S.W. 107th Avenue, Miami, FL 33174   305-559-6715

HAWAII
1143 Bishop Street, Honolulu, HI 96813   808-521-2731

ILLINOIS
172 North Michigan Avenue, Chicago, IL 60601   312-346-4228

LOUISIANA
4403 Veterans Memorial Blvd, Metairie, LA 70006   504-887-7631

MASSACHUSETTS
885 Providence Hwy, Dedham, MA 02026   781-326-5385

MISSOURI
9804 Watson Road, St. Louis, MO 63126   314-965-3512

NEW YORK
115 E. 29th Street, New York City, NY 10016   212-754-1110

SOUTH CAROLINA
243 King Street, Charleston, SC 29401   843-577-0175

TEXAS
No book center; for parish exhibits or outreach evangelization, contact: 210-569-0500, or SanAntonio@paulinemedia.com, or P.O. Box 761416, San Antonio, TX 78245

VIRGINIA
1025 King Street, Alexandria, VA 22314   703-549-3806

CANADA
3022 Dufferin Street, Toronto, ON M6B 3T5   416-781-9131

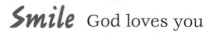
Smile God loves you